Please consider returning this book or leaving
another book in it's place.

54 Ironstone Drive Little Free Library in
Elizabethtown, PA

My sister and I first heard the story of Clever Tortoise when we were small. We lived in East Africa then, in Tanzania. We thought it was a new story (because _we_ had just heard it), but it was an old story that the Ngoni people of southern Tanzania would tell each other.

Making this book of it, all this time later, the bush came flooding back to me—its different lights and smells, the animals and insects, the colors of lake water, the ground that is so interesting when you have only little legs.

NYOKA
snake

I have put some Kiswahili words into this version of the story. I hope you will not find them difficult. It is the language most widely spoken in Tanzania. The sound of it in my ears makes me remember other sounds of East Africa—like storm rain drumming, cicadas singing, and the noise of two little girls laughing over the clever trick that Clever Tortoise played on the banks of Lake Nyasa. I hope you will laugh too . . .

Francesca Martin

CHUNGU
black ant

CLEVER TORTOISE

A traditional African tale

Francesca Martin

CANDLEWICK PRESS
CAMBRIDGE, MASSACHUSETTS

NYUKI
bee

NGIRI
warthog

KISUNGURA
rabbit

KOBE
tortoise

PANYA
rat

MJUSI
lizard

CHURA
frog

Listen!
There is a lake in Africa, called Nyasa.
Mmm, it is full of blue cool water.

On the banks of Nyasa live
Rabbit, Warthog, Lizard,
Hippopotamus, Snake, Elephant,
Chungu — the little black ant —
and many other animals.

Clever Tortoise lives there too.

See? Everyone is happy now.
But once there was a quarrel.
Hm, tch, tch, it started like this . . .

"See how big I am?"
cried Elephant one day.
"I am stronger than all of you
little animals!"

And a great big
elephant-sized crashing
and trampling
and spoiling
and stamping
began in the bush by Lake Nyasa.

Ooh, tch, tch, it was bad.

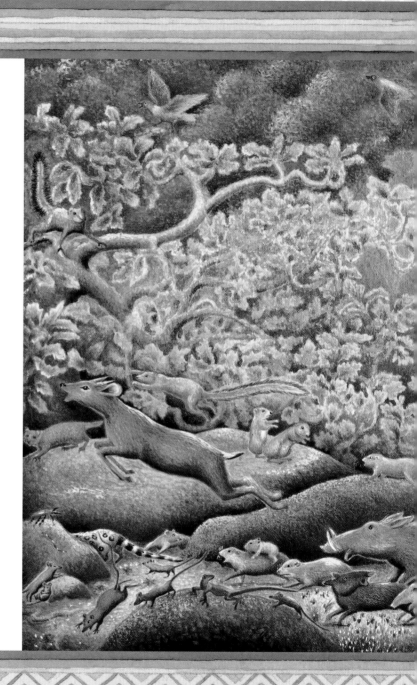

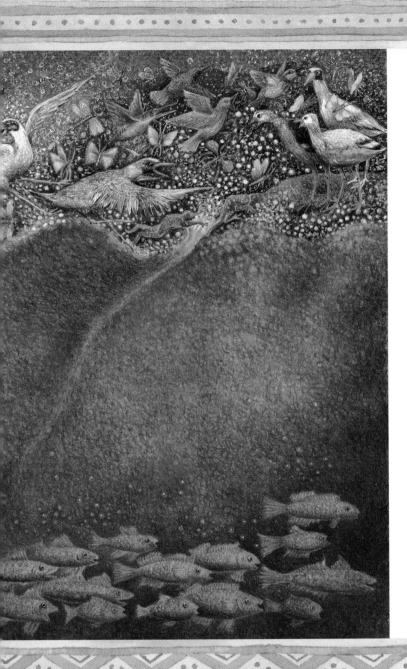

Hm, and it was catching.

"See how huge I am?" cried
Hippopotamus another day.
"I am stronger than all of you
small animals!"

And a great huge
hippopotamus-sized
splashing
and bubbling
and churning
started in the waters of Lake Nyasa.

Aah, tch, tch! It was worse.

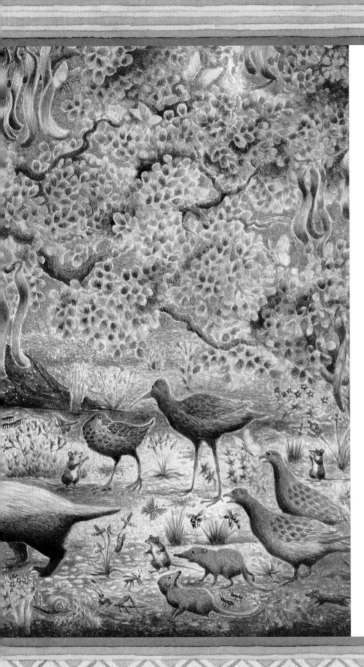

Rabbit, Snake, Lizard, and the others
grew frightened.

Warthog called a meeting.
"What shall we do?" he asked.
"That Elephant and that
   Hippopotamus are bullies."

All the animals thought.

Clever Tortoise thought too.
Ahh! that tortoise. His head is small,
but his brains are big and strong.
"Ha!" he said, after just a little time.
"Let's play a trick on them . . ."

Pitter-patter, pitter-patter.
Clever Tortoise led the others
through the bush to find Elephant.

"Mr. Mighty Elephant," Clever Tortoise
called. "I hear you are the strongest.
Will you fight a tug-of-war with me?"

"You?" snorted Elephant.
"A little teeny tortoise?
Fight a tug-of-war with ME!"

"Yes," said Clever Tortoise. "I will
meet you right here at sun-up
tomorrow, with a rope."

Pitter-patter, pitter-patter.
Then Clever Tortoise took the others
to the water to find Hippopotamus.

"Mrs. Fine Hippopotamus," Clever
Tortoise said. "I hear you are the strongest.
Will you fight a tug-of-war with me?"

"You?" scoffed Hippopotamus.
"A weeny small tortoise?
Fight a tug-of-war with ME!"

"Yes," said Clever Tortoise. "I will meet
you right here at sun-up tomorrow,
with a rope."

That night, Clever Tortoise,
Rabbit, Warthog, Lizard, and
the others stayed awake.

My! What rustling and tying,
what rolling and twisting,
what knotting and plaiting
of long strong tree vines there was —
all through star time.

To weave one long strong rope.

Ha!

The sun rose,
and the blue cool water
of Lake Nyasa
turned to red and gold.

Elephant rose too.

"Good morning, Mr. Elephant,"
Clever Tortoise said. "Will you
take this end of our tug-of-war
rope? Then we can begin."

"Huh!" snorted Elephant.
"I will pull you over quicker than
a hummingbird beats its wings!"

But where do you think
Clever Tortoise and his friends
went with the *other* end of their
long strong rope?

Ha!

"Good morning, Mrs. Hippopotamus,"
Clever Tortoise said. "Will you take
this end of our tug-of-war rope?
Then we can begin."

"Humph!" snorted Hippopotamus.
"I will pull you over faster
than a frog can jump!"

But that boastful Hippopotamus
and that proud Elephant,
they had one enormous surprise
coming their way . . .

"NGGHHHHH!"
grunted Elephant.
"MMMMMPH!"
groaned Hippopotamus,
as the tug-of-war began.

"OOOOOOOF!"
moaned Elephant.
"AI-AI!" gasped
Hippopotamus,
as the tug-of-war went on.

And each of them thought,
"This teensy tortoise,
he is very strangely
STRONG."

The sun climbed high
and higher in the sky,
till there was not one
shadow left in all Africa.
Ooh, and it was hot.

But still the rope stayed tight.

"Enough!" said Clever Tortoise.
And he cut the rope
with a little stone ax.

Well, what do you think
happened then?

CRASH! fell Elephant,
and he bumped his big strong head.

SPLASH! fell Hippopotamus,
and she smacked her broad great back.

Pitter-patter, pitter-patter.

Clever Tortoise went to visit Elephant in the bush.

"Quicker than a hummingbird beats its wings?" he called.

Elephant just stared at that teeny tortoise.

Where did he hide his strength? In his toes?

Pitter-patter, pitter-patter.

Clever Tortoise went to visit Hippopotamus by the water.

"Faster than a frog can jump?" he called.

Hippopotamus just gazed at that weeny tortoise.

Where did he hide his strength? Underneath his shell?

That night, Elephant and
Hippopotamus slept a deep
tired tug-of-war sleep.
But the smaller animals stayed awake.

My! What clapping and swinging,
what dancing and jumping
happened in the moonlight!

"You clever Clever Tortoise!" cheered
Rabbit, Warthog, Lizard, Snake,
Chungu — the little black ant — and all
the others. "That was one good trick!"

And that's how that quarrel was mended.

See? All the animals are happy again.

Kwa heri ya kuonana, wanangu —
so long, children, till we meet again.

For my sister, Philly

*I would like to thank Helen Read for
the decorative borders she has designed and
painted so beautifully, and Lucy Ingrams,
whose ideas have brought rhythm and
humor to the text.*

First U.S. edition 2000

Library of Congress Cataloging-in-Publication Data

Martin, Francesca.
Clever Tortoise : a traditional African tale / illustrated by Francesca Martin.
p.   cm.
Summary: Clever Tortoise leads the other jungle
animals in teaching bullying Elephant and Hippopotamus
a lesson by tricking them into engaging in a tug of war with each other.
ISBN 0-7636-0506-9
[1. Folklore — Tanzania.]   I. Title
PZ8.1.M368C1   2000
398.2′09678′0452792—dc21   [E] — 99-047080

2 4 6 8 10 9 7 5 3 1

Printed in Hong Kong

This book was typeset in Throhand Ink.
The illustrations were done in watercolor.

Candlewick Press
2067 Massachusetts Avenue
Cambridge, Massachusetts 02140